The Terrible Truth

The Terrible Truth

Stephen Roos

Illustrated by Carol Newsom

A Yearling Book

Published by
Dell Publishing Co., Inc.
1 Dag Hammarskjold Plaza
New York, New York 10017

Yearling ® TM 913705, Dell Publishing Co., Inc.

ISBN: 0-440-48578-9

Reprinted by arrangement with Delacorte Press

Printed in the United States of America

First Yearling printing—March 1984

CW

For Frank E. Taylor

AUTHOR'S NOTE

Readers of *My Horrible Secret* will remember that made-up names were used to protect the identities of the parties involved. Because the revelations in this book may prove equally painful to certain individuals, the author has decided to stick with the made-up names.

Contents

1 The Day Before the Day After Labor Day   1

2 The First Day   9

3 "Big Plans"   21

4 Steps in the Right Direction   29

5 The New Kid   35

6 Her Best-Laid Plans   45

7 Welcome to the Club!   51

8 Things Go from Worse to Worst   61

9 Down and Out in New Eden   67

10 The Last-Ditch Effort   73

11 To Forgive Is Not Divine   81

12 The Terrible Truth   89

13 Even Bad Things Come to an End   97

14 The Dance   105

15 What Happened Last   113

The Terrible Truth

1

The Day Before the Day After Labor Day

According to the calendar, the summer ends and fall begins the third week of September, but kids in the very small town of New Eden know better. Fall begins the day that school starts. And in New Eden school starts the day after Labor Day.

Labor Day always falls on the first Monday in September, when the lawns are still green and the leaves on the trees haven't given a single thought to turning orange and gold and calling it quits until next spring. The most you can do is pray that the first Monday in September will fall on the fifth or sixth of the month. If you pray really hard, Labor Day may even fall on the seventh.

The year Shirley Garfield started the sixth grade Labor Day fell on the first day of September. All of August everyone who went to New Eden Middle School complained about how it was just another typical example of how life is so unfair to kids. One of them, Randy Pratt, even circulated a petition demanding that the calendar be changed. Shirley was practically the only kid who hadn't signed it. All her life she had been looking forward to sixth grade. As far as she was concerned, sixth grade couldn't start soon enough.

Outside it was a glorious late-summer day. The sky was crystal clear and the temperature was perfect too, but Shirley was too engrossed in her preparations for the first day of school to care or even to notice. As the clock on the church steeple two blocks away struck eleven, Shirley sat at the small white desk in her bedroom double-checking. Everything was in order: ten pencils, all new; five felt-tipped pens, also new; two spiral notebooks, never before touched; and a wooden ruler into which Shirley had carved not only her name but also her address and telephone number just in case she lost it somewhere.

From the patio below Shirley could hear the voices of the women from one of her mother's clubs. It wasn't her mother's garden club, Shirley knew, because the garden club always met in the living room. It was her mother's bridge club that met in the garden when the weather was nice. But, of course, the bridge club wasn't playing bridge today. On Labor Day the bridge club always had a picnic after the town softball game.

Shirley stood up and looked out her window. The women on the patio were already setting out things for the picnic, which meant it was time for Shirley to go downstairs. She took one more glance at all her school things laid out neatly on the desk and made double sure that all the stripes on her bedspread were absolutely straight before she went out into the hall and ran down the stairs. When she got to the kitchen, her mother was standing at the sink scraping carrots.

"Is there something I can do to help?" Shirley asked.

"I think everything's under control, dear," her mother said as she threw the scrapings into the garbage. About twice a day, and this was one of those times, Shirley decided she had the most wonderful mother in the world. First of all, Mrs. Garfield was the best-looking mother in New Eden. But more than that she was also the nicest. Some girls want to be just like their mothers when they get married and have children of their own. Not Shirley. She wanted to be just like her mother now.

"Maybe I could help set out the forks and knives and stuff," Shirley suggested.

"Mrs. Pratt's already taking care of that," Mrs. Garfield said.

"Then maybe I could get the charcoal grill going? I know how to do that," Shirley said.

"I'm afraid Mrs. Winfield is working on that right now," Shirley's mother said. Shirley was so eager to help that her mother felt almost apologetic about not having anything for her to do.

Shirley thought for a moment. "The salads," she said. "I could put them out on the picnic table."

"Oh, we don't want to put them out in the sun until

everyone gets back from the softball game," Mrs. Garfield said. "We wouldn't want them to spoil."

"Then there's nothing for me to do?" Shirley asked wistfully.

Shirley's mother put her arms around Shirley and hugged her. "There's plenty you could be doing," she said. "You could go meet Dad at the softball game. Everyone's welcome to play."

"I'd rather not," Shirley said. "I wouldn't want to get my clothes dirty."

Mrs. Garfield smiled. It wasn't the first time in the last few months that Shirley had amazed her mother with her tidiness. "You don't have to play," Mrs. Garfield said. "You could watch, you know."

"I don't think so, Mom," Shirley said.

"But you should be outside having fun. It's your last day of summer vacation."

Shirley thought it over for a second. For as long as she could remember she had gone to the Labor Day softball game with her father. The last two years she had even played in it. But this year was different. The softball game was mostly for the little kids, and Shirley was too old for that sort of thing now.

"I don't think I'll go, Mom," she said. "Even to watch."

"Well, I don't want you moping around the house on such a lovely day. Okay?"

"I promise, Mom," she said. "I'm not going to be moping. As a matter of fact, there's something very important I just remembered. When does the picnic start?"

"In about an hour, I guess," Mrs. Garfield said. "The same time it starts every year."

"Fine. I'll see you in an hour."

Without waiting for her mother to say anything more about going outside and having fun, Shirley left the kitchen and ran back up the stairs to her room. What Shirley had to do was a lot more fun than a softball game.

She opened the door to her closet. Even though she had gone over everything in it a dozen times a day for the last three weeks, what she saw still brought a big smile to her face. There, hanging before her, were all the wonderful new clothes that she was going to wear this year. Of course, she wasn't the only person in New Eden with a closet full of clothes. Everyone had clothes, but Shirley had a real wardrobe. As anyone can tell you, the difference between having clothes and having a wardrobe is planning. And Shirley had been planning her wardrobe all summer.

That meant no more jeans. No more little-girl dresses, either. The dresses and the jumpers and the blouses and the skirts were the prettiest and the most grown-up that Shirley had ever had. The best part was that she had a different pair of shoes for every day of the week and a little purse to go along with them.

Of course, everyone in New Eden knew that Shirley liked to carry a purse, but last year she had had only one. This year she had five, which meant she was never going to have to repeat. If it was Monday, Shirley was going to wear the red shoes and take along the red purse. On Tuesday she would have the blue shoes

and the blue purse. On Wednesday it was going to be yellow. Thursdays were for green and Fridays were for the beige.

This year Shirley was going to look like a grown-up. She was going to act like one too. For one thing, she had promised herself to be a lot more organized about her homework. This fall she was going to have it all done and out of the way by the time dinner was ready. After dinner she was going to take care of the dirty dishes without fail. With all that done, she could spend as much time as her mother and father let her talking on the phone to the other girls in her class, just the way girls in high school do. And before she went to bed at night, she was going to take her comb and her chewing gum and her change from one purse and put them all neatly into the purse that she would be using the next day.

As Shirley stood staring at all her wonderful clothes and thinking all her wonderful thoughts, she heard cars pulling up in front of the house. The softball game must be over now. Within seconds her father and all the other fathers and all the children would be invading the house for the picnic.

It was time to go downstairs. But even as she closed the closet door one more time and walked into the hall, Shirley's mind wasn't on the picnic at all. All she could think about was tomorrow. Tomorrow was going to be better than Christmas, she thought. Better than a birthday too. Tomorrow Shirley was going to become an adult.

2

The First Day

Because it was Tuesday, Shirley wore the blue shoes and carried the blue purse to her first day of sixth grade. The night before she had wavered a little, but a plan was a plan. Shirley knew that she had to stick by her decisions no matter what.

When Shirley went downstairs for breakfast, her parents were already there.

"Good morning, Pumpkin," her father said as he took a sip of his coffee. "You look as pretty as a picture for your first day of school."

"As pretty as a *pretty* picture?" Shirley asked.

"A *very* pretty picture," her father said.

Shirley smiled even though her father had said it to her a million times before. It was the best way to start a day, she thought. This day especially.

"What do you want for breakfast?" Shirley's mother asked.

"I'm too excited to even think of food, Mom," she said.

"You're not going out of the house without breakfast," her mother said.

"Okay. I give in. But just juice and cereal."

Shirley sat down next to her father.

"Can I give you a lift to school?" her father asked. "Or are you too excited to ride in the car?"

Shirley smiled. "I think I'll walk, Dad. I might see some of the other kids on the way."

"And they might see you too."

This time Shirley blushed a little. Her father always knew exactly what she was thinking. Sometimes it was nice, but other times it was a little embarrassing.

Shirley gulped down her breakfast as quickly as she could. Then she kissed her mother and father and left the house. Just because she had plenty of time didn't mean she wasn't in a hurry.

Unfortunately, almost everyone else in the sixth grade was wearing new clothes too, or at least new hand-me-downs. No one had much interest in anyone's clothes but their own. Most of the kids had new book bags too, except for Claire Van Kemp who was carrying a real briefcase. Claire was wearing a pair of faded blue jeans but Shirley couldn't tell if they were new faded jeans or old faded jeans.

The only person who definitely wasn't wearing new clothes was Miss Presley. Miss Presley's dress was very nice, but Shirley remembered it from last year when Miss Presley had been their fifth-grade teacher.

"Welcome to the sixth grade, children," Miss Presley said. "I'm glad to see that all of you who were with me last year are here again. And I'm happy to see a new face here, too. You'll all get to meet Gaylord soon enough. Welcome, all of you."

"And congratulations to you, Miss Presley, on your promotion to sixth grade," Randy Pratt said. "Did you have to pull a lot of strings?"

"Just lucky, I guess," Miss Presley said, but she didn't look as though she felt very lucky at all. Maybe the battle between Warren Fingler and Claire Van Kemp the spring before had made fifth grade something that Miss Presley was still trying to forget. "By the way, boys and girls, my name isn't Miss Presley anymore."

"What happened to your old name?" Randy Pratt asked.

Miss Presley smiled for the first time since she had told the students to take their seats. "Nothing happened to it, Randy," she said. "It's just that I'm Mrs. Simkins now."

There was a hush.

"You mean you and the gym coach?" Warren Fingler asked.

"That's just what I mean, Warren," the former Miss Presley said. "Mr. Simkins and I were married at the beginning of August. So in a way you don't have exactly the same teacher you had last year. Let me write my new name on the blackboard for you."

She picked up a piece of yellow chalk and wrote "Mrs. Simkins" on the blackboard, which was really green, but everyone called it the blackboard anyway.

One of the best things about Mrs. Simkins was that she always wrote without making those horrible screeching noises that a lot of the other teachers made.

As soon as she finished, the class started to clap, Shirley included. Two rows in front of her, however, Shirley saw someone who wasn't clapping. It seemed he wasn't even paying attention. It was the new boy, Gaylord. Even if he wasn't being very polite, Shirley decided that he looked sort of cute from the back at least because his hair was neatly combed and he was wearing a nice sweater.

"That's enough, boys and girls," Mrs. Simkins said. "But I want to thank you very much."

"Well, now that we know what you did over the summer," Claire Van Kemp said, "I suppose you'll all want to know what I was up to."

"I'd rather do the new math," Randy Pratt said. "It can't be any worse than the old math."

Most everybody in the class laughed. Claire Van Kemp thought she could run the school just because her family seemed to run almost everything in New Eden.

"Well, since I was president of the fifth grade and will probably end up being president of the sixth grade, I think it's my duty to go first," Claire said.

"You mean you're actually going to permit elections this year?" Warren Fingler asked.

Mrs. Simkins rapped the pointer on the edge of her desk. "Please, Warren, let's have some order. We don't want a repeat of last year, do we?"

"Mrs. Simkins," Claire said, this time raising her hand as she spoke. "I just thought everyone would be interested to know about the lunch I had with the governor after I won the contest to raise money to restore the head on the statue of Matthew Bumkis on the village green. Did everyone see my picture in the paper? It was on the first page, but I have Xerox copies for anyone who missed it."

There was a groan from the class. This time Shirley raised her hand. Unlike Claire Van Kemp, however, she waited until Mrs. Simkins called on her before she spoke up.

"Yes, Shirley?" Mrs. Simkins asked. "Would you like to add something?"

"Well," said Shirley. "I for one would be interested in hearing about Claire's meeting with the governor."

"And I for two would be very interested in knowing what Claire and the guv had to eat," Randy piped up. "I guess it can't be any worse than the new math, right?"

"We had sandwiches in the governor's office," Claire said. "He had tuna on whole wheat with lettuce and mayo and I had bologna on white bread with lettuce and mustard."

"He didn't even bother to take you to a restaurant or something?" Warren Fingler asked.

"It was a working lunch, Warren," Claire said. "The governor and I had a lot of things to discuss."

"What did you talk about?" Mrs. Simkins asked.

"We talked about organization, Mrs. Simkins,"

Claire said. "The governor told me that even when he was a little boy, he was always organizing clubs and things. He said it helped him to get a head start over the other kids when it came to being a grown-up."

Shirley Garfield raised her eyebrows. Something Claire said had clicked in her mind. "Just what sorts of things did the governor organize when he was a child?" she asked.

"Why, all sorts of things," Claire replied. "When he was eight, he organized a club that cleaned up trash from vacant lots in the city where he grew up. And when he was eleven, he got the kids in his school to put on a play and they gave all the money they got for it to the poor people. When he was twelve, he won a Jaycee's contest and when he was fourteen, he won an award for being the best Boy Scout in the state and when he was fifteen, he—"

"I think we get the picture," Mrs. Simkins interrupted. "The governor sounds like an exemplary individual."

"Well," Claire said. "I'd just like to add that the governor was always president of his class just the way I am, and don't forget I won a Jaycee's contest too. The governor said I was a credit to the boys and girls of our state, Warren."

"So why don't you just sit back and rest on your laurels?" Warren asked. "You don't want to burn yourself out before you get to be a teen-ager, do you?"

"One thing that none of us at the top of the heap can afford to do is rest," Claire said. "The governor and I see eye to eye on that too."

"Well, Claire, you might want to give some of us at the bottom of the heap a rest," Randy Pratt said. "Why don't you just proclaim yourself president for life and get it over with once and for all?"

"Well, I wouldn't go that far," Claire said thoughtfully. "The governor and I are very much in favor of regular elections. It's more democratic that way."

"But the governor always runs against somebody," Warren said. "The only time you ran against someone it was Patsy Conklin and you lost. You got to be president because Patsy's family moved out of town and no one else would run against you."

"Yeah," Randy said. "I don't see why we bother having elections at all."

Shirley raised her hand and waited for Mrs. Simkins to call on her. "But if we don't have elections," she said, "then we wouldn't have any president at all."

"That's the way it works," Claire said. "No elections, no president."

"After all, it's not Claire's fault that no one runs against her," Shirley said. "It's not her fault that an election with only one candidate isn't really an election. No one can blame Claire for that."

"My sentiments exactly," Claire said. "Why don't we have the election right now? Maybe in a couple of years someone somewhere will run against me. In the meantime I'm perfectly happy to run unopposed. Mrs. Simkins, would you like me to pass out the ballots?"

Before Warren or Randy could protest, Mrs. Simkins rapped the pointer against the edge of the desk again, only this time a lot more firmly than she had before. "Please, class," she said. "We're not going to have elections yet."

"We're not?" asked Claire. "We always have elections the first day of school."

"I'm sorry, Claire, but what Shirley said is right."

"What Shirley said?" Claire asked incredulously. "Shirley didn't say anything about no elections."

"That's right, Mrs. Simkins," Shirley said. "I didn't say anything."

"Yes, you did, Shirley," Mrs. Simkins said. "You said that an election with only one candidate isn't really an election. Unless there are at least two candidates for president of the sixth grade, there aren't going to be any elections this year. Is there anyone who would like to run against Claire Van Kemp?"

Twenty-eight pairs of eyes peered around the room to see if there was anyone who would.

"Is there anyone you would like to nominate for president?" Mrs. Simkins asked.

Again, the twenty-eight pairs of eyes roamed around the classroom. When they had gone from the front of the class to the back where Claire sat, they saw one hand go up.

"Yes, Claire?" Mrs. Simkins asked. "What do you want to say?"

"I'd like to nominate someone," she said.

"Someone besides yourself?"

"That's right, Mrs. Simkins."

"It's highly irregular for one candidate to nominate another," Mrs. Simkins said.

"If it means the difference between having an election and not having one, I'd like to nominate Shirley Garfield."

"You want to nominate *me?*" Shirley gasped. "Why would you do something like that to *me?*"

"You got me into this mess," Claire said. "Now you get me out of it."

"But I don't want to be president of the sixth grade," Shirley said. "I didn't mean to get you in a jam."

"If you run against me," Claire said, "I'll let you be my friend forever."

"What if I win?" Shirley asked.

"Don't worry," Claire said. "You don't have a chance."

"Just because I don't want to win an election doesn't mean I want to lose one," Shirley said. "Besides, I've got big plans this year. Mrs. Simkins, I am very happy to announce that I refuse the nomination."

"Are there any other nominations?" Mrs. Simkins asked as she looked around the room for a raised hand. No one stirred. "Well, I guess we're not going to have an election. Not this year."

"You can't do this to me, Shirley Garfield," Claire said. "I'll never forgive you for ruining my political career."

"And I'll never forgive you for trying to make me

do something I didn't want to do in the first place," Shirley said.

For what Mrs. Simkins hoped was the last time that morning, she pounded the pointer on her desk. "Please, Claire. Please, Shirley. Please, everyone. Let's open our spellers to page one."

Silently, the boys and girls did as they were told. Whether they liked it or not, sixth grade had begun.

3

"Big Plans"

Shirley had been a sixth grader for less than an hour and already she had done something very grown-up. She had not let Claire Van Kemp push her around, which was more than a lot of the other kids could say. As far as Shirley was concerned, she had good reason to be pleased with herself.

After Mrs. Simkins recessed the class for lunch, Shirley saw there was an empty seat at the table where the musketeers were eating. That was the collective name everyone used for Margie Neustadt, Kimberly Horowitz, and Gracie Arnold.

Each of the musketeers had lived in New Eden all her life, but the truth was that no one in school knew them very well. That was because the musketeers had become best friends on the first day of the first grade and they had stayed that way ever since. If Mrs. Simkins hadn't insisted that the students in her class sit in alphabetical order, the musketeers would have been sure to sit together. They always spent the afternoons together, sometimes they did their homework together. On Saturday afternoons they went to the movies and once a month their parents let them have a slumber party.

Even though Kimberly Horowitz had red hair and lots of it and Margie Neustadt had brown braids and Gracie Arnold had black hair, which she wore in a ponytail, Shirley decided that the musketeers had begun to look like each other over the summer. Shirley guessed it was because each of the musketeers had an older sister, which meant that Kimberly and Margie and Gracie had to wear hand-me-downs. As far as Shirley was concerned, all hand-me-downs looked alike. Shirley could only thank her lucky stars that her mother and father had had the foresight not to give Shirley an older sister.

"So what did you girls do over the summer?" Shirley asked as she put her tray on the table.

"I went to Camp Kadota for three weeks and then I came home," Margie said.

"How about you, Kim?"

"Oh, I went to Camp Kadota for three weeks and then I came home."

"And you, Gracie?" Shirley asked. "Camp Kadota for three weeks and then back to New Eden?"

"Who told you?"

"Just a lucky guess," Shirley said.

"What about you, Shirley?" Kimberly asked. "What did you do all summer? Did you go away to camp?"

"I was thinking about it," Shirley said, "but I decided I was getting a little too old to go to camp anymore."

"Well, I loved Camp Kadota," Gracie Arnold said. "They make you do a lot of things there like swim and play tennis and make potholders so it was a lot of fun."

"A lot of fun," Kimberly added.

"The best summer we ever had," said Margie. "So what *did* you do, Shirley?"

"I had a summer job," Shirley said.

All three musketeers said "ah" at exactly the same time. Shirley knew they were impressed.

"Actually, I had two summer jobs," she added.

"Two?" asked Gracie. "How did you manage that?"

"Well, they were both part-time jobs," Shirley said modestly. "One was doing the window displays for Mrs. Fingler over at the Book Worm. The other job was reading to the little kids at story hour at the library."

"Did you get paid?" Kimberly asked.

"Sort of," Shirley said. "Mrs. Fingler gave me one hardcover book or three paperback books each time I did the windows. The library work was free. It's a charity."

"Are you going to have a job this fall?" Margie asked. "Is that your big plan?"

"Big plan?" Shirley asked. "What big plan?"

"You said you couldn't run for president because you had big plans," Margie said. "Aren't you going to let us in on them?"

"Oh, *those* big plans," Shirley said. "I'm afraid I can't discuss them now. They're secret."

The musketeers nodded.

"But you'll tell us sometime, won't you?" Kimberly said.

Shirley nodded back at the musketeers, hoping that they wouldn't realize that the "big plans" were just something she had said to get Claire Van Kemp off her back. "When I'm ready to tell, you'll be the first to know. What with my summer jobs and getting all my clothes in order, I just haven't had time to get the plans—*final.*"

Shirley knew she probably shouldn't have mentioned her clothes. She didn't want the musketeers to feel bad just because they didn't have to worry about new clothes.

"I love your new outfit," Margie said. "Especially the purse and the shoes. Who cares what Claire Van Kemp says."

Shirley felt the blood rise in her face. "Claire?" she asked. "What did Claire say?"

"Nothing worth paying the slightest bit of attention to," Margie said. "On the way to lunch Claire said your clothes were frivolous. But you know Claire. Who cares what she thinks?"

"I don't care at all what Claire thinks," Shirley said. "It's what she says that's the problem."

"What do you think of the new boy, Shirley?" Gracie Arnold asked, trying to change the subject. Shirley had begun to look very, very unhappy.

"Gaylord? The one who sits in the front row?" Shirley asked. "I hardly noticed him."

"You hardly noticed him?" Kimberly asked in alarm. "Margie and I are both jealous of Gracie because she gets to sit right next to him on account of her last name being Arnold and his last name being Adamson."

"What's so great about sitting next to him?" Shirley asked.

"We've decided that he's sort of dreamy," Kimberly said.

"He looked okay from the back," Shirley admitted. "What's he like from the front?"

"He's fantastic," Margie said. "He's better looking than Greg Stockard even."

"What color eyes does he have?" Shirley asked.

"Gee, I haven't the faintest idea," Kimberly said. "I haven't seen him from the front either, but Gracie's seen him from the side . . ."

"The right side," Margie said.

"The right side," Kimberly confirmed. "And she says he's out-of-this-world-looking."

"From the right side only," Gracie said. "I couldn't get him to look at me full face. Maybe this afternoon I'll get a better look."

"And you'll give us a full report," Kimberly said.

"You know I will," Gracie said. "Unless Shirley sees him first. Then she has to give us a full report."

"But I sit two rows behind you," Shirley said. "It's not very likely that I'll see him first."

"But you're going to be seeing Gaylord all the time,"

Gracie said. "He lives practically next door to you."

Shirley was startled. "There's no one named Adamson on my street," she said. "And no one's moved in or out for ages, and I should know."

"No you wouldn't," Kimberly said. "But I would."

"How would you know when I don't?" Shirley asked. She didn't mean to sound harsh, but Shirley and her mother kept very close tabs on their neighbors.

"Because my mother is Mrs. Skillman's best friend and your mother isn't," Kimberly said. "It's as simple as that."

"If it's as simple as that," Shirley said, "how come I don't understand a word you're saying?"

"Because your neighbor Mrs. Skillman is Gaylord's aunt and that's why I know everything about him even though I don't know what he looks like exactly."

"He's my neighbor?" Shirley asked. "He's staying with the Skillmans?"

"That's right," Kimberly Horowitz said.

"Is he an orphan?" Shirley asked.

"My mother says he's almost an orphan," Kimberly said.

"You mean his parents are dying right now?" Shirley asked.

"No," Kimberly replied. "His parents are alive and kicking, but my mother says that her friend Mrs. Skillman says that Gaylord might as well be an orphan for all the attention his parents pay him."

"What's wrong with Gaylord's parents?" Shirley asked.

"Well," Kimberly said, lowering her voice so that the other three had to move in closer to hear what she was saying. "Mrs. Skillman doesn't like to be critical of anyone, especially of Gaylord's parents because, after all, Gaylord's mother is Mrs. Skillman's own sister, but even Mrs. Skillman has to admit Gaylord didn't have a very happy childhood."

"Are his parents mean to him?" Gracie Arnold asked.

"Oh, they don't hit him or anything," Kimberly said. "But they move around a lot. My mother told me that Mrs. Skillman told her that in the last three years Gaylord has lived in fourteen different places and gone to eleven different schools. Isn't that sad?"

"What's the matter with his parents?" Shirley asked. "Can't his father hold down a job?"

"Oh, it's nothing like that," Kimberly said. "Gaylord's parents are terribly rich. They don't even have to work for a living. So whenever they get bored with where they're living, they just move on. That's why Gaylord has come to live with his aunt and uncle. So that he can stay put for a while. Isn't that nice?"

"Only if he's as cute from the left side as he is from the right," Gracie Arnold said. "I just hope the sides of his face match."

"I'm sure they will," Shirley said. "They usually do."

"Well, my mother once knew someone . . ."

It wasn't that Shirley wasn't interested in what Gracie was saying, but already her mind was a million miles away. Suddenly she knew just what her "big plans" were.

Just because she hadn't meant to say anything about "big plans" didn't mean she wasn't honor-bound to think some up. Besides, "big plans" were a large part of what being a grown-up was all about.

All the little details like who and how and when and where and what still had to be taken care of, but Shirley was already plotting her first steps. And her first steps were going to be in the direction of the Book Worm, which everyone in town called the Worm.

4

Steps in the Right Direction

Shirley lived only five blocks from New Eden Middle School, which was why she walked to school while almost all the other students took the bus. Sometimes she rode her bike, but usually she walked because it took only ten minutes. Besides, it didn't seem very grown-up to be riding a bicycle. Once her purse strap had got stuck in the bicycle chain and it had taken Shirley two hours to get the grease off.

This afternoon, however, she wished she had brought her bike to school. If she had, she could have made it to Warren Fingler's mother's bookstore in no time at all. On foot it took her almost half an hour to get there.

Shirley opened the door to the store and heard the little bell above announce her arrival. In one corner was an old man looking over the travel books. The only other person was Mrs. Fingler at the little table in the front with the cash register on it.

"Why, Shirley," Mrs. Fingler said. "It's so nice to see you. I didn't expect to see you the first day of school."

"Well, you know how it is," Shirley said, not sure at all what she meant by it. "I was in the neighborhood."

"Look all you want, Shirley," Mrs. Fingler said. "I just got a new shipment of paperbacks. I bet you'll find something you'll want."

"Well, Mrs. Fingler," Shirley said. "I'm not really looking for a book this afternoon. I'm looking for something more along the lines of stationery."

"Stationery?" Mrs. Fingler said. "I wish I could get Warren or Roger to write a letter."

"I'm not really looking for the kind of stationery that you write letters on, Mrs. Fingler," Shirley said. "I was looking more for the sort you send out invitations on."

"You know where it is, Shirley."

Mrs. Fingler led Shirley to a rack where there was row after row of cards for birthdays and christenings and for people who were in the hospital and for kids who were graduating from high school.

Shirley studied the little packets of invitations on the top row. Some of the cards read, "We're having cocktails and you're invited" or "Guess whose birthday it is?"

"I'm not having a cocktail party," Shirley said. "And it's not my birthday yet."

"Well, we have invitations for almost every occasion," Mrs. Fingler said. "What's your occasion?"

"I'm afraid I'm not at liberty to divulge that," Shirley said. "At least not yet, if you know what I mean. I was sort of hoping you'd have something very simple. Without anything written on it.

"Maybe these little white cards would be nice," Mrs. Fingler said. She handed Shirley a little box filled with small white pieces of paper and envelopes to go along with them.

"I think that would be just fine, Mrs. Fingler," Shirley said. "At least for now. I'm not really sure how big my occasion is going to be yet."

"Well, if it gets bigger, you can always come back for more," Mrs. Fingler said.

"I guess that's a possibility," Shirley said. "How much does that come to?"

Mrs. Fingler looked at the package. "That'll be a dollar thirty-three with tax. Shall I put it in a bag for you?"

"I wish you would," Shirley said as she opened her purse and handed the money to Mrs. Fingler. "It's not that I'm doing anything wrong, of course, but it's sort of a surprise."

"A secret surprise?" Mrs. Fingler asked as she handed Shirley the paper bag and change.

"I guess you could call it that," Shirley said. "Mrs. Fingler, I was just sort of wondering . . ."

"You were wondering if maybe I wouldn't tell anyone that you were in my shop today, I bet."

"That's sort of what I was wondering," Shirley said. "I just wouldn't want to ruin the surprise, you know."

"Don't worry, Shirley," Mrs. Fingler said. "Wild

horses couldn't drag it out of me, especially since I haven't a clue what your secret surprise is. If anyone asks, I'll tell them I haven't seen you in weeks."

"Thanks, Mrs. Fingler," Shirley said. "I knew I could count on you."

Shirley put the pennies in her purse and let herself out into the street. Now she had to decide what step two of her big plan was.

In a way it was a good thing that Shirley had to walk all the way home that afternoon. By the time she got to the door of her own house, she knew exactly what she was going to write on the invitations.

Even though she had promised herself that she was going to make it a rule to have all her homework done by dinnertime, she tossed her book bag on her bed and sat down at her desk. Nothing was going to get in the way of what Shirley knew she had to do now.

Very carefully, she took the box of stationery from the paper bag and slipped the writing paper and the envelopes from the box.

She began to write:

YOU ARE CORDIALLY INVITED
TO A TOP SECRET, DON'T-TELL-A-SOUL
MEETING
AT 304 MAPLE AVENUE

Shirley paused. She hadn't yet decided when she should have this meeting. Tomorrow would be too soon, she thought. The people who were getting the invitations weren't getting them until tomorrow at noon, and most of them probably wouldn't know they had received them until that afternoon or maybe that evening. So tomorrow was out. So was Thursday. Mrs. Garfield's garden club would be meeting at the house Thursday afternoon. Friday was better, Shirley thought. Her mother would be at the hospital being a Pink Lady.

Just below the 304 Maple Avenue part, Shirley wrote:

AT 4:00, FRIDAY, SEPTEMBER 5ᵀᴴ

Shirley looked at the invitation. As far as she was concerned, it was perfect. It was very mysterious and the handwriting was excellent too. She wrote out two more invitations exactly like it. She folded each very neatly and put it in an envelope. Then she licked the envelopes and sealed them shut.

The only thing left to do was to address the envelopes. On one envelope she wrote "K.H." for Kimberly Horowitz. On another she wrote "M.N." for Margie Neustadt and on the third she wrote "G.A." for Gracie Arnold.

By tomorrow afternoon the musketeers would be a part of Shirley's big plan. But even they wouldn't have the slightest idea of what it was.

5

The New Kid

"Your homework assignment will be to solve the problems on page eight of your math text," Mrs. Simkins said.

"When do we have to turn the answers in, Mrs. Simkins?" Randy Pratt asked.

"Tomorrow morning would be fine," Mrs. Simkins said.

"I was sort of hoping for next Monday," Randy said. "Then we could have the whole weekend."

"Don't worry, Randy," Mrs. Simkins said. "I'll find some other assignment for you to spend the weekend on."

Randy was about to go into his usual groan when the bell rang. They all closed their math books and rested them on their desks, but no one stood up to go to lunch. Mrs. Simkins didn't allow anyone to leave the room without her permission, bell or no bell.

"Okay, boys and girls," she said. "You can go to the

cafeteria now. When we get back to class, we'll be doing our American history and our science."

Everyone rose and headed for the door. Shirley knew that Mrs. Simkins would wait until they were on their way before she went off to have her own lunch in the teachers' lounge.

Shirley tagged along behind the others as they walked down the corridor. When they reached the cafeteria, Shirley doubled back to the girls' room, where she washed and dried her hands three times just in case someone came in. Then she left the girls' room and retraced her steps back to the classroom.

Shirley peered through the window in the door. There was no one there. She turned the doorknob. It was unlocked and she heaved a sigh of relief.

She walked into the classroom and closed the door behind her. She went to her desk and pulled out the envelopes.

She looked at the first one. "K.H." Kimberly Horowitz sat right next to Shirley. Shirley went to Kimberly's desk and opened the math text to page eight. She dropped the envelope on the page, closed the book, and put it back exactly where Kimberly had left it.

The next envelope was for "M.N." Margie Neustadt sat directly behind Kimberly. Shirley went to Margie's desk and slipped the second envelope onto page eight of Margie's math book. Now Shirley had just one more envelope to deliver.

She walked to the front of the classroom where

Gracie Arnold sat. For a moment Shirley wasn't sure if Gracie sat two or three seats from the end of the aisle. She remembered that Stanley Aarons sat in the first seat because no one ever went before Stanley, at least not alphabetically. So Gracie had the second seat. Shirley picked up Gracie's math book and slipped the last invitation into it.

She walked quickly to the door and let herself out into the corridor. There was no one there, coming or going. When it came to doing grown-up things, great planning was everything.

Shirley was in such a state of excitement that afternoon that she couldn't have told you what she had for lunch even while she was eating it. And she certainly couldn't have told anyone what she was learning that afternoon about Jamestown and Plymouth Rock, or anything at all about how tadpoles turn into toads. Or maybe it was frogs they turn into.

The hardest part about embarking on a major secret project was that you had to be absolutely calm, cool, and collected. Otherwise, someone was bound to suspect something, which wouldn't do at all. When everyone knew about Shirley's plan and she became the most popular and admired girl at school, she wanted everyone to be as astonished as a tadpole is when it turns into a toad. Or a frog.

Shirley couldn't keep her mind on anything except her secret until she was walking home, her book bag slung over her left shoulder and her yellow purse (because it was Wednesday) slung over her right shoulder.

It was only when she got to the stoplight at the corner where Maple Avenue meets Elm Street that she noticed Gaylord, who had been walking ahead of her. Even Shirley had to admit his was the best right side of a face she had ever seen. Shirley had been so engrossed in her secret plan that she probably wouldn't have noticed any side of him if he hadn't been every bit as cute as Gracie Arnold had said he was.

"You're Gaylord, aren't you?" she asked. "You don't know who I am, I bet, but I sit three rows behind you in Mrs. Simkins's class. My name is Shirley Garfield."

He turned to her. "Yeah, I'm Gaylord," he said. Even though he had a pretty grim expression on his face, Shirley had to admit that it was a pleasure to see all of it. Gaylord Adamson had wavy blond hair and what Shirley's mother called perfect features. The only thing about him that wasn't perfect was his smile. Gaylord didn't seem to have one.

"I'm Shirley Garfield," Shirley said.

"You already told me that," Gaylord said. "Do you know how long it takes for this light to turn green?"

"It stays red for exactly ninety seconds, but it stays green for only forty-five," Shirley said. "I counted last year."

"Was it a school project or just your idea of a good time?" Gaylord asked, but Shirley knew it wasn't a question. It was just a way for Gaylord to be mean.

"Well, I walk to school every day except when the

weather's really bad, and I walk home every afternoon unless I've got something else to do, of course, and I wondered why the light always takes so long to change so I brought along a stopwatch one day just so I could find out. It wasn't any big deal, but you said you wanted to know."

Before Shirley could say another word, the light turned green and Gaylord started to cross the street. If Shirley could have walked in the opposite direction, she would have. But this was her way home too, and she wasn't about to let the new kid scare her away. By the time Gaylord had made his way to the next block, Shirley was walking beside him again.

"I hope you don't mind the company," she said.

"It's a free country, isn't it?"

"That's what they say," Shirley said. "It must be hard getting used to living in a new town."

"Hardly," Gaylord said. "I've lived in more new towns than you can imagine. I'm doing okay."

"That's what Kimberly Horowitz told me," Shirley said.

"What's a Kimberly Horowitz," Gaylord asked.

Shirley refused to let Gaylord bait her. "Kimberly Horowitz is a very nice person and she sits next to me in Mrs. Simkins's class, which is probably why you haven't seen her yet, but her mother is a very good friend of your aunt and that's how come I know you've lived all over the place and that's how I know we live practically next door to each other. I live at Three-oh-four Maple and the Skillmans live at Three-oh-eight.

Anyway, I hope you get to like New Eden once you've settled in."

"I guess stranger things have happened," Gaylord said. "But I'm probably not going to be hanging around here that much longer."

"But Kim said you were living with the Skillmans on a sort of permanent basis now on account of your parents traveling all the time."

"My parents are living in Switzerland now," Gaylord said. "They'll probably want me to go over later on when the skiing gets good."

"Did they tell you that?"

"Not in so many words," Gaylord said. "But they will."

"Maybe they think it's better for someone your age, our age I mean, to stay put for a while. It must be rough going to a lot of different schools."

"That's what my uncle and aunt seem to think," Gaylord said.

"Don't you like the Skillmans?" Shirley asked.

"They're nice enough, I guess," Gaylord said. "I just don't know how long I'll be able to survive in a one-horse town like New Eden."

"What do you mean, one-horse town?" Shirley asked.

"I mean a place where there's nothing to do," Gaylord answered. "You know, a real hick town."

"It's not a hick town. It's a very nice town. I've lived here all my life and I've enjoyed every moment of it," Shirley said, even though she knew that wasn't anywhere near the truth.

"If you like talking to trees, I suppose."

"There are people here too," Shirley said. "Nice people."

"Like that girl, Claire what's-her-name, who's always shooting off her mouth?"

"Well, some people are nicer than others," Shirley said. "Besides, it's Claire Van Kemp. It's two words but it's one last name."

"At least she seems to have a little spunk," Gaylord said. "Everyone else around here is too quiet. I'm used to a little more excitement."

They were just a few feet from the gate to Shirley's front yard. As far as Shirley was concerned, it wasn't near enough.

"This is where I live," Shirley said. "I'm sorry we won't be able to get to know each other any more today. I've got a lot of things to do this afternoon."

"Don't sweat it," Gaylord said. "It's no big deal my not being crazy about your town. I'm sorry if you took it the wrong way."

Shirley said nothing. She opened the gate and walked up the brick path to the front door of her house. Only when she got to the steps did she look around. Gaylord was already turning in at the Skillmans' house.

Her mother had said more than once that you must never judge people by first impressions, but this time she wasn't going to pay attention to her mother's advice. Gaylord Adamson was a very rude and very mean boy. Shirley was almost sorry that she had tried to be nice to him.

By the time she had let herself into her house, she had even decided that Gaylord Adamson wasn't all that good-looking either.

By the time Gaylord had turned into the Skillmans' front yard, he was already feeling rotten about the way he had talked to Shirley. He wondered why he was always meanest to the people who tried to be nice to him. Like his aunt and uncle. Like Shirley Garfield.

Gaylord reached under the door mat for the key that his aunt always left for him. As he bent over, two books he had been holding in his other hand fell to the ground. Gaylord picked up the books. From one of them, his math text, fell an envelope. There was nothing written on the back of it and Gaylord turned it over.

There were his initials, "G.A.," on the front. Gaylord dropped his other books and opened the envelope. Inside was the invitation to a "top-secret, don't-tell-a-soul meeting" on Friday. He knew who had sent him the invitation, too, because 304 Maple Avenue was Shirley Garfield's house.

The girl he had been so mean to had sent him a secret invitation. In all the schools he had ever gone to no one had ever invited him to something special.

On Friday afternoon, when he got to Shirley's house, he was going to do something he never considered doing before.

Apologize.

6

Her Best-Laid Plans

Shirley wasn't exactly sure that her mother's living room was the best place for a top-secret, don't-tell-a-soul meeting. The problem was that the room was so pretty that no one would think it was in the least bit mysterious. The den was a possibility but there was a television in it and Shirley was afraid that one of the musketeers would want to watch it instead of paying attention to the very important announcements that Shirley was to make that afternoon.

The kitchen was definitely out because it was the kitchen, and the back yard wasn't even a possibility because you never could tell who might sneak up on you when you weren't looking. Secret things had to be done indoors. Everyone knew that.

The only other place Shirley could have considered for her secret meeting was the attic. The afternoon after Shirley had passed out the invitations, she went up to the attic and decided that it was all wrong for what she had in mind.

Shirley admired the way her mother kept everything nice and neat. In fact, she had every intention of doing the same when she grew up. But in a way she was disappointed to see that her mother's attic was as immaculate as all the other parts of the house. In other houses where Shirley had visited the attics, Shirley had been intrigued by the dusty floors and dirty windows, the debris from the Christmas decorations and the old clothes that people didn't want to wear again but didn't have the heart to throw out.

In Shirley Garfield's mother's attic the floors were covered with checkerboard linoleum that was polished once a month and the windows at either end had curtains that had been made especially for them. Along the sides were cupboards and closets and built-in drawers. The attic was the envy of all the other mothers in New Eden, but for once Shirley wished she could build a sloppy old attic on top of her mother's tidy one and have her secret meeting there.

When Shirley got home from school on Friday afternoon, she had resigned herself to the fact that the living room was the only place she could hold her first meeting. Maybe later the girls would be able to suggest other places to meet. Maybe if they were lucky, they could even arrange to have a secret meeting place, a place that no one would know about for sure, but everyone would whisper about.

She went directly to the kitchen and opened the refrigerator. She took out the plastic bottle of Coke and rummaged through the bread box for cookies she had set aside for the day's festivities.

Ordinarily, Shirley preferred the kind of cookies that had a little layer of chocolate on the outside and a large glop of marshmallow on the inside. The cookies that Shirley was serving today were called English tea biscuits. They were very small and came in three different shapes and didn't taste like anything much at all. Still, they would be perfect for her purposes.

Shirley opened the box of cookies and spread them out on one of her mother's good dinner plates. There were still enough cookies to fill up another plate, but she decided to put the others back in the box. If the girls wanted more, she would bring out the rest. But not until the musketeers had finished the first plate.

Shirley unscrewed the top of the Coke bottle. Only a little foam dripped down to the counter before she could stop it. Back at the cupboard she reached for her mother's large silver pitcher and emptied the bottle into it.

Everything was perfect, except for the fact that the soda would be warm by the time the girls arrived. Shirley tried to put the pitcher into the refrigerator, but there wasn't enough room. She thought a bit and reached into the freezer for a tray of ice. She emptied the whole thing into the pitcher.

When her mother entertained the women from the bridge club or the garden club, she didn't bring out the refreshments until the end of the afternoon. Shir-

ley wasn't going to take any chances that the musketeers might think she wasn't going to offer them
anything. When they got to her house, they were going
to see right away that she hadn't stinted on her hos-
pitality.

Very carefully, because the Coke came almost to
the rim of the pitcher, Shirley carried it into the living
room and set it out on the coffee table in front of the
big couch. Then she went back to the kitchen for the
cookie plate, which she put down next to the pitcher.

Shirley went back to the kitchen and found four of
her mother's special glasses and brought them to the
living room. When she had put them down on the
coffee table, she knew the only thing left to do was
worry.

Shirley's mother had explained it to her once. Before
a party you were always anxious because there was
always the possibility that no one would come. Maybe
they had not received their invitations. Maybe they
had received the invitations but had decided not to
come. Maybe they had decided to come but had had
an accident on the way. For all Shirley knew, one or
all three of the musketeers might be lying in the
Emergency Room of New Eden Memorial Hospital.

Which meant that at this very moment Shirley's
mother was serving the musketeers fruit juice from
plastic cups while Shirley should have been serving
them Coca-Cola from a silver pitcher. But there were
worse possibilities: The musketeers might have laughed
at the whole idea of the secret. They might tell every-

one at school about it, and then everyone in the world would be laughing at her too.

For a moment she felt very cross with the musketeers, especially with Kimberly Horowitz because everyone knew that Kimberly was the biggest gossip in town.

Shirley tried to calm down, but she couldn't. She was too nervous about what would happen if her plan failed and too excited about what would happen if it worked out. In fact, she didn't know what she would have done if at that very moment, when the clock on the mantel said it was exactly four o'clock, the doorbell hadn't rung. Shirley raced to the window to see who it was. Kimberly Horowitz stood on the doorstep.

Good old dependable Kimberly, Shirley thought as she went to answer the door. Kimberly was someone you could always trust, and Shirley thanked her lucky stars that she had had the wisdom to invite her.

Shirley opened the front door just a crack.

"It's me, Shirley," Kimberly whispered. "I'm not late, am I? It's Kimberly."

"You're not late," Shirley whispered back. "How do you know I'm Shirley?"

"Because you've always lived at Three-oh-four Maple," Kimberly whispered.

"Okay," Shirley said as she opened the door wide. "Are you alone?"

"Of course I am," Kimberly said. "I didn't breathe a word about this to anyone, not even Gracie or Margie."

"Good," Shirley said. "Come in but make it quick. I don't want the whole town to see."

Within a second Kimberly was standing in the middle of the living room and Shirley had shut the door.

The big plans had begun.

7

Welcome to the Club!

Shirley decided to reward her first arrival with permission to take one English tea biscuit from the plate as long as she didn't disturb the design of the cookies. When Kimberly took the first bite from the cookie (which was also her last because the cookies were so small), the doorbell rang again.

Without waiting to excuse herself, Shirley went to the door and opened it. Now she was in so much of a hurry to get things started that she opened the door all the way. In the doorway stood Margie Neustadt with her invitation in hand.

"Three-oh-four Maple Avenue," Margie said. "Here I am. Am I the first to arrive?"

"You're right in the middle," Shirley said as she gestured for Margie to come in.

"Oh, Kimmy," Margie said. "I didn't know you were going to be here. You told me you were spending the afternoon at your grandmother's."

"And you told me you were taking your bike in for

repairs," Kimberly said. "I guess we're both pretty good at keeping top secrets, aren't we?"

"I guess so," said Margie as she sat down on the couch next to Shirley. "I'm in the middle so that means there's one more person coming. Am I right, Shirley?"

"You guessed right," Shirley said.

"Will you tell us who else is coming?" Kimberly asked.

"You can guess but I'm not going to tell you," Shirley said. "Have an English tea biscuit, Margie."

Margie took a look at the plate on the coffee table.

"May I have two?" Margie asked. "They're a little on the small side."

"You may have all you want," Shirley said. "But one at a time, please."

Margie took a cookie and ate it in one bite.

"What's in the pitcher?"

"Coca-Cola," Shirley said.

"Are the glasses for the Coke or are they just for decoration?"

"They're for when everyone gets here," Shirley said emphatically.

"Are you going to tell us what's top secret?" Margie asked. "Or do we have to wait until the third person gets here?"

"Well, I think we should wait," Shirley said. "It's only polite, don't you think?"

"But Gracie's never on time," Kimberly said. "Why do we always have to wait for her?"

"What makes you so sure it's Gracie who's coming?" Shirley asked.

"Well, who else?" Kimberly asked. "You asked me and you asked Margie and you said there are three of us, so who else would you invite?"

"You did invite Gracie, didn't you?" Margie asked. "I'd feel awful about being in on something unless Gracie was in on it too."

"Especially since both Margie and I are in on it," Kimberly said. "It would hurt poor Gracie's feelings if she weren't. She's very sensitive, you know. Her mother says that's why she's always late for things."

"Because she's so sensitive?" Shirley asked.

"That's right," Kimberly said. "So why don't you go ahead and tell us what the meeting is all about?"

"You can tell Gracie when she gets here," Margie suggested.

"If it *is* Gracie, of course," Kimberly said. "If it's not, I'm not sure I want to hear about it at all."

Shirley had a feeling that if she thought long and hard enough about what Kimberly was saying, she might understand. But since Gracie *was* the third person, it didn't seem to matter much one way or the other.

"So what's the secret?" Margie asked as she took another cookie. There was something about the way she bit into it that told Shirley she couldn't stall any longer.

"Well, the secret is that I'm starting a club and I want the three of you to be charter members," Shirley said.

"A club?" Kimberly asked. "What's so secret about a club?"

"It's a secret club," Shirley said. "Anyone who becomes a member has to take a vow of absolute secrecy. You can't tell anyone you're a member and you can't tell anyone who the other members are either. You can't tell anyone when or where we meet and you can't tell what we do at all our meetings. It's a secret from start to finish."

"Oh, Shirley," Margie said. "That's the most exciting thing I've ever heard. I promise I won't tell a soul, except Kimmy and Gracie, but that's okay because they'll be members too."

"Only if they decide they want to join," Shirley said. "If they don't want to join, you'll have to keep mum about all the secret things we'll be doing."

"What kind of secret things *will* we be doing, Shirley?" Kimberly asked. "And how many members are there going to be and who are they going to be? And who's going to be president of this thing anyway?"

"I'm glad you asked those questions," Shirley said as she leaned forward on the couch. "I think any club has to have officers, don't you? I never heard of one that didn't have a president anyway. And I want you to know that I'm perfectly willing to be president. Of course, we can elect someone if you'd prefer."

"You're going to be our first president?" Kimberly asked.

"Well, it was my idea to have a secret club," Shirley said a little defensively. She didn't want anyone to get the idea that she was trying to be another Claire Van Kemp. "I just thought that it would be appropriate for me to volunteer."

"And do you get to decide who all the members are?"

"Oh, no," Shirley said. "We all get to decide. Whenever we meet someone who would make a good club member, everyone gets to vote. But we all have to vote yes. Just one vote can keep someone out. It's what they call a blackball. It's supposed to be a lot of fun."

"If I'm already a member, I guess it's a lot of fun," Margie said.

"Oh, yes," Shirley said. "All the charter members are in for keeps, but everyone else has to take their chance."

"What's the club do that's so secret?" Kimberly asked.

"Aw, come on, Kimmy," Margie said. "It's more exciting if it's secret. Then everyone will want to join in."

"If it's a secret, I don't see how anyone is going to know there's anything to join," Kimberly said.

"Don't be silly," Margie said. "Someone's bound to suspect something. Right, Shirley?"

"That's perfectly correct," Shirley replied. "My mother says that when she was in a secret club at college, that's exactly what happened. Nobody knew what the name of the club was and nobody knew what the club did, but everyone on campus knew there was a club and everyone wanted to join."

"It sounds logical to me," Margie said.

"Well, I still want to know what this club does," Kimberly said.

"I'm afraid I can't tell you anything else unless you promise to be a member," Shirley said.

"That's not fair," Kimberly said. "Just tell us something."

Shirley thought it over. "I can tell you two of the club's rules," she said.

"Shoot," said Kimberly.

"The first one is that no boys are allowed. That's because we're going to have a sorority just like the one my mother was in at college. Sorority comes from Latin and it means no boys."

"What's the other rule?" Kimberly asked.

"Well, it's absolutely and positively the last thing I can tell you, until we're all official members, of course."

"It better be good," Kimberly said. "I'm not sure I like the idea of a sorority that doesn't allow boys."

"How would you like to join a club that doesn't allow Claire Van Kemp?" Shirley asked.

From the expressions on Kimberly's and Margie's faces, Shirley could tell that she had won them over.

"A club without Claire?" Kimberly asked. "Would it be in the bylaws?"

"An excellent suggestion," Shirley said.

"Okay," Kimberly said. "You're on. I'll join anything that Claire can't get into."

"Me too," said Margie.

Shirley heaved a small sigh of relief. For the first time that afternoon it looked as if her plan was as foolproof as she had hoped. Shirley took a cookie and sat back on the couch to enjoy her moment of triumph. The doorbell rang.

"That's Gracie," Margie said. "I can't wait to tell her about the club."

"I think you'd better let me do the honors," Shirley said as she stood up to go to the door. "After all, it was my idea in the first place."

Shirley opened the front door. There, where Gracie Arnold should have been standing, was Gaylord Adamson.

"I'm sorry I'm late," he said. "But my aunt wanted me to run an errand for her and I didn't know how to say no since I knew this afternoon's a secret."

"Secret?" Shirley asked in dismay. "I'm not sure I know what you're talking about?"

"If you don't know what the secret is, then who does?" he asked as he pulled the invitation from his pocket. "It's four o'clock, isn't it? And this is Three-oh-four Maple Avenue, isn't it? And this is the envelope you put inside my math book, isn't it?"

Gaylord showed the envelope to Shirley. There they were, the initials, "G.A.," just as Shirley had written them. A horrible tremor went through Shirley's entire body. With a dreadful rush she understood why Gracie Arnold hadn't shown up: The initials for Gracie and for Gaylord were the same, and it was all Shirley's fault that Gaylord had received Gracie's invitation.

"I'm sorry I was so mean to you the other day," Gaylord was saying. "I was sorry even before I found the invitation in my math book. You were trying so hard to be nice and I was trying so hard to be mean. You're the first person who ever wanted me to be in on a secret," he said as he took a step into the living room.

Shirley tried desperately to explain the situation to Gaylord but the words stuck in her throat. She was too upset to look him in the face. Instead, she looked above his head and then over his shoulder and saw something that suddenly made everything even worse.

Turning in at the gate and stalking up the brick path was Claire Van Kemp. Shirley didn't have to look twice to know that Claire Van Kemp was mad as a hornet.

8

Things Go from Worse to Worst

"I just knew it!" Claire Van Kemp bellowed. "I should have suspected all along that something was up!"

As Claire stomped into Shirley Garfield's living room, Gaylord jumped aside to get out of Claire's way and Shirley stood as still and stiff as a statue. In another second Kimberly and Margie were on their feet.

"What did you know?" Kimberly asked, almost as though she wished that Claire hadn't heard her question.

"I knew you were all up to no good," Claire screamed.

"I don't know what on earth you can be talking about," Shirley said, fighting hard to recover her composure. "I can have some of my friends over after school, can't I? I don't need your permission for that."

"You're up to some secret plot," Claire said. "I knew it as soon as I left the dentist's office."

"The dentist?" Shirley asked. "I don't see what any of this has to do with teeth. Your teeth especially."

"It has everything to do with my teeth," Claire said firmly. "This afternoon, right after school, my mother took me to Dr. Feiner's office for my semiannual cleaning and checkup. After I had the usual news that I didn't have a cavity in my head, I was walking through the waiting room when who should I see but little Gracie Arnold sitting there crying her little eyes out. So I went over to her and told her that a dental appointment wasn't anything to be afraid of and she started crying even harder. So I said to her how come you don't have the other musketeers around to hold your hands."

"The musketeers?" Kimberly interrupted. "Who are the musketeers?"

"Oh, that's what everyone in town calls the three of you," Claire said. "On account of the fact that you guys are always hanging out together. Didn't you know that?"

"I never heard that," Margie said, sounding a little wounded. "Everyone in town calls us that, you say?"

"It's a small town," Claire said. "Ask your friend Shirley here if you don't believe me."

"Is it true, Shirley?" Margie asked.

"Only behind your backs," Claire replied before Shirley had a chance to say anything. "Anyway, once

I explained who the musketeers were to Gracie, she started crying even harder. She said she knew the two of you were up to something behind her back and that was why she was so upset. So when my mother was driving me home from the dentist and I saw Kimberly standing outside your house, Shirley, I figured something fishy was going on. So I got my bike and rode over here and sure enough, there was Margie at the door."

"Nothing fishy is going on," Shirley said. "Nothing that concerns you."

"Everything in this town concerns me," Claire said. "Shirley Garfield's dirty tricks especially."

"But I didn't mean to hurt Gracie," Shirley said. "It's all a horrible mistake."

"But you told us you sent Gracie a secret invitation too," Margie said. "You lied, Shirley."

"I didn't lie," Shirley said. "You've got to understand. I goofed."

"You don't have to tell *me* that," Claire said. "You goofed and how."

"That's not what I meant," Shirley said. "I did put an invitation in Gracie's math book, but I guess it was Gaylord's math book. It was a mistake. And because his initials are the same as Gracie's, he thought it was for him."

Gaylord moved toward Shirley. "You mean it's not?" he asked. "You mean you really didn't want me to be part of the secret?"

It was all too much for Shirley. Without bothering

to ask her guests, invited or not, to sit down too, Shirley collapsed into the wing chair by the fireplace.

"Let me see that," Claire said, pointing to the envelope Gaylord was holding.

In less than a second Shirley was back on her feet. "Don't show it to her, Gaylord," she pleaded. "It's private."

"Not anymore," Claire said as she grabbed the envelope from Gaylord. Claire took the invitation from the envelope and read it. "Top-secret, don't-tell-a-soul meeting," she read. "Just what I thought. You're up to no good."

"I am not," Shirley said.

"It's just a club," Margie said.

"A secret club," Kimberly added.

"No boys," Margie said.

"And no Claire Van Kemp," Kimberly added.

"No boys?" Gaylord asked.

"No Claire Van Kemp?" asked Claire Van Kemp. "You mean you've already decided that you don't want me to be a member?"

"I was hoping you wouldn't take this personally," Shirley said.

Claire dropped the invitation and the envelope on the floor. "I can understand your not wanting boys in the club," she said. "If you're starting a club, you've got to draw the line somewhere. But not letting me into your club is out of the question. You've lived in New Eden long enough to know that, Shirley."

"If I live in New Eden for a hundred years, I won't

know that. If I want to start a club, I can. I can have anyone I want as a member, whether you like it or not."

"Lots of luck, Shirley," Claire sneered.

"Don't be so sure of yourself," Shirley said. "Lots of people will want to join my club. Just ask Margie. Or ask Kimberly."

Claire put her hands on her hips and looked each of the girls in the eye. "Look here, musketeers," Claire said, breathing very deeply. "Your dearest friend in the world, Gracie Arnold, lies this very minute in a dentist's chair crying her little heart out because of Shirley Garfield and her secret club. Look at Gaylord here," she continued, pointing in Gaylord's direction. "Gaylord is a stranger in a strange town. He's a newcomer who doesn't have a friend in the world. And look at the kind of welcome Shirley Garfield has given him."

Margie looked at Kimberly and Kimberly looked at Margie. Then they both looked at Claire.

"We didn't want to hurt anyone's feelings," Margie said. "Not Gaylord's and certainly not Gracie's. We just thought it would be sort of nice to join a secret club."

"Maybe it wasn't such a good idea after all," Kimberly said. "I'm sorry, Shirley, but it looks like we're not going to join your secret club."

"But you can't mean that," Shirley said. "I'll explain the mistake to Gracie and she'll want to join as much as you and Margie did. Everything's going to be fine.

The secret club's going to be the most fun we ever had."

"But it's not going to be much of a secret anymore, is it?" Margie asked. "I mean what with Claire and Gaylord knowing about it, how can it be?"

"An excellent point," Claire said. "It looks like you've got yourself a secret club that isn't a secret, Shirley. Plus it's the only club I ever heard about that doesn't have any members either."

"It's all a misunderstanding," Shirley said. "I didn't mean to hurt anyone's feelings. I just wanted us to have some fun after school. That was all."

"Well, maybe you'll think up a better way to go about it next time," Claire said. "If there is a next time, that is."

Claire walked to the front door and opened it. "Come on, Margie and Kimberly. Come on, Gaylord. I don't think there's anything left to do around here."

The two girls followed Claire first. Then Gaylord. Claire held the door for the three of them. "There are a lot of other things we can do instead," Claire said as they started down the steps toward the front gate. "Why don't we all go over to my house and talk about it?"

Just as Claire was shutting the front door behind her, she turned back to Shirley.

"Have a nice day, Shirley," she said. And then she closed the door.

9

Down and Out in New Eden

The ice in the silver pitcher had melted and the Coca-Cola was watery and flat. Shirley took the glasses and the pitcher to the kitchen and left them in the sink. She went back to the living room for the plate that held the cookies. Even with all the excitement Kimberly and Margie had been able to devour all but one of them. Surrounded by a few crumbs, the lone cookie looked as lost and forlorn as Shirley felt.

She threw the cookie in the garbage and poured the Coke down the drain. She put the glasses and the plate in the dishwasher and rinsed the silver pitcher and rested it upside down on the drainer beside the sink.

Now the house looked as if there hadn't been a meeting at all. With all her heart Shirley wished that were true. She felt sorry at what she had done to Gracie and Gaylord, and she felt bad for Margie and Kimberly too.

What it all came down to was the fact that she didn't have a friend in the world. What made it worse was that she never was going to have one either. By Monday morning everyone at school would know what happened. No one would ever speak to her again.

Shirley wondered what the rest of her life was going to be like. Maybe Mrs. Simkins would call on her in class now and then, maybe even ask her to go to the blackboard and parse a sentence. But since Mrs. Simkins was paid for her work, it didn't really count.

In a year or two Shirley wouldn't remember how to carry on a conversation. By the time she was in high school, she probably would be unable to make sounds. When she grew up, she was destined to be one of those people who walk along the sidewalks, grunting away, while all the world passes by, uncaring, uninterested. Shirley was well on her way to being the kind of person only a mother could love.

Her mother. The thought of her mother made her feel a little better. Her mother would speak to her. And Shirley would tell her mother all about the secret club and how she had made one little mistake in delivering the invitations and how everyone was going to make her pay for it the rest of her life.

Her mother would kiss her on the forehead and tell her there was nothing to worry about. Her mother would make everything all right again.

She looked at the clock on the mantelpiece. It was only four thirty, which meant her mother would be home from being a Pink Lady at the hospital in another hour. An hour wasn't usually a very long time for Shirley, but right now it was longer than an eternity.

She picked up the beige purse that she had left on the table by the front door. She opened the door and took her bike out of the garage. It was almost two miles from Shirley's house to New Eden Memorial and there was no time to walk it.

She rode along Maple Avenue and turned onto Elm Street. There wasn't any traffic and there weren't any other kids on their bikes either. Things were already beginning to look up. It wasn't until Shirley got to the hospital parking lot and was locking the chain of her bike around the tree that she saw a familiar face.

The face was Warren Fingler's. He was walking toward the hospital entrance, and it was too late for her to duck behind a tree. He had already spotted her.

"Hi, Shirley," Warren said. "You're not sick or anything, are you?"

"If I were sick or anything, I wouldn't have been able to ride myself to the hospital," she said. "I'm here to see my mother."

"Gee, Shirley," Warren said. "I didn't know she was in the hospital. How long has she been sick?"

"My mother's not a patient," Shirley said. "She's a Pink Lady three days a week. What are you here for?"

"My checkup," Warren said. "With Dr. Bradley."

"Checkup?" Shirley asked. "Is something wrong with you?"

"He just wants to see my arms," Warren said.

"Your arms?" Shirley asked. "What's wrong with your arms?"

"Don't you remember?" Warren asked. "You know. My left arm and my right arm? Last spring? The riding accident and the baseball game?"

Shirley had to think a bit before she did remember. Warren had broken both his arms, one when he had fallen off a horse and the other when he had backed into a fence while he was trying to catch a baseball. For a while it had seemed that people in New Eden were talking about nothing else but Warren Fingler and his broken limbs.

"Of course I remember," Shirley said. "I guess I've just got a lot on my mind today."

"That's okay," Warren said. "I didn't expect anyone was going to remember forever. Even in New Eden. I guess everyone's just waiting around for the next major happening so they'll have something else to talk about."

"What major happening?" Shirley asked.

"Well, I won't know until it happens, will I?" Warren said. "Something's bound to happen sooner or later."

"Maybe not," she said hopefully. "Almost nothing ever happens in New Eden. That's one of the nicest parts about living here, don't you think?"

Warren frowned. "I don't know," he said. "It doesn't take much in this town to get everyone talking."

She shuddered a bit. Not for Warren because he was yesterday's news. Shirley was shuddering for herself because she had a feeling that she was going to be tomorrow's.

"I don't want to make you late for your appointment with Dr. Bradley," she said, hoping that Warren would take the hint and go away.

"Well, actually," he said, "I'm a little early."

"You never know, Warren. Sometimes Dr. Bradley finishes early. You wouldn't want to keep him waiting."

Warren got the hint. "I'll see you around, Shirley," he said.

She watched him walk into the building and down the hall toward the doctor's office. Then Shirley went around to the other entrance and walked toward the room where the Pink Ladies took their breaks. No one was there so she sat down to wait.

Warren hadn't meant to make things worse. Still, what he had said made her more anxious than ever. She tried not to think about him or Claire or Gaylord or Gracie or any of them, but she couldn't help herself.

If there had been a magazine anywhere, she would have picked it up and tried to read. But there wasn't anything to read. There wasn't anything on the walls to look at either, so Shirley gave in to all of her sad, self-pitying thoughts.

She didn't know how long she had been staring into space before she realized that her mother was standing in the doorway.

"Shirley?" she said. "I didn't know you were coming over this afternoon. What a nice surprise!"

Her mother looked as pretty as she always did in her dress with the pink and white stripes. Shirley tried to say something but the words wouldn't come. She tried to look at her mother but little blurs that might have been something like tears kept getting in the way.

Before she knew what she was doing, she was running to her mother and holding her tight. She was crying out loud now, and there was no way for her to pretend that she wasn't.

For the first time since she had been a very little girl, Shirley Garfield felt like one.

10

The Last-Ditch Effort

"You *are* going to tell me about it, aren't you, dear?" Mrs. Garfield asked once they were home. "You can't spend the rest of your life crying."

Shirley swallowed hard and wiped away the tears from her eyes and cheeks. Slowly she began to explain about the club and about how she had gone about sending out invitations and about how she had made the mistake and then about how everything had exploded in her face that afternoon. When Shirley got to the bitter end, her mother was just putting the last jar in the cupboard.

"Why didn't you tell me about your plan?" Mrs. Garfield asked as she sat down in the chair next to Shirley's.

"I wanted it to be a secret," Shirley said. "But just at first. I was going to tell you when it was all set up and then you would have been proud of what I'd done."

Mrs. Garfield put her hand over Shirley's. "I'm

proud of you already, dear," she said. "Why do you think you need a club to make me proud?"

"You have the garden club and the bridge club and the Pink Ladies," she said, looking her mother in the eye, hoping she would understand.

"The Pink Ladies aren't a club, Shirley."

"They are sort of," Shirley said. "You get to wear special clothes. You belong to things and everybody likes you and looks up to you. I want that too."

"They're different from your club," Mrs. Garfield said. "Your club was to keep people out as much as it was to get people in. If you don't like Claire very much, wouldn't it have been easier just to tell her?"

"Claire's very pushy and she thinks my clothes are frivolous, Mom," Shirley said. She decided to let her defense rest on that. "So what do you think I should do?"

"I think you're going to have to decide for yourself," her mother said.

"Can't you give me a hint?" Shirley asked.

"I could. I could even tell you what to do step by step. But it wouldn't do you any good."

"I'd do exactly what you want me to do," Shirley pleaded. "I promise."

"I know that, dear, but that's not the point. You're getting to an age when you're going to have to make your own mistakes and you're going to have to learn from them too. It won't mean anything if you do what I tell you. You won't learn anything from it."

"But you're making it so hard on me, Mom. I need help."

"Someday, when you're my age, I hope you'll see what I'm talking about," Mrs. Garfield said. She put her arm around Shirley's shoulder and drew her near. "Do you believe me?"

"I believe you, Mom," Shirley said. "It's just hard for me to understand."

"You will," Mrs. Garfield said. "In time."

Shirley decided to wait until her father came home from work. He was sure to come up with a solution, but she was wrong. As he sat in his armchair and listened to everything that had gone wrong, he nodded sympathetically but he didn't say a word.

"Aren't you going to tell me what to do, Dad?" she asked when she had finished.

"I think your mother's right," he said.

"About figuring it all out myself?" she asked.

"You're old enough," he said. "And I know you're bright too."

Shirley nodded her head, but not very enthusiastically. It was nice, she supposed, that her parents always got along so well, but there were times when she wished they didn't always agree with one another.

Shirley thought it over. She thought it over at dinner that night and she thought it over at least eight different times on Saturday. By Sunday night, when she was setting out her clothes and her red purse and her red shoes for Monday morning, Shirley had thought it over another dozen times and still didn't have an idea of what she was supposed to do.

Maybe the best thing was to write Claire a note of apology, Shirley thought. She sat down at her desk and pulled a piece of paper from the top drawer. It was the same notepaper that she had used for the invitations. She winced at the thought but she started to write something about being sorry for everything that had happened and promising that it would never happen again. When she got to the part about hoping that she and Claire could be friends, she crumpled up the piece of paper and threw it in the wastebasket.

It was no use. She didn't want to be Claire Van Kemp's friend for anything in the world. Besides, if she wrote a note of apology to Claire, she would have to send another one to Gaylord. And another to Gracie. And Margie. And Kimberly too. With her luck all the letters would fall into the wrong hands.

It would be much better if she just asked the principal to give her free air time on the school's public-address system. Or maybe she could take out an ad in the newspaper. Or maybe she should stand in the middle of the playground and let all the kids throw rocks at her for half an hour. If they wanted to, they could even make faces at her and laugh at the way she dressed. On second thought she decided she would prefer it if they just threw rocks and left her clothes out of it.

Shirley still wasn't sure about anything when she and her parents were having breakfast the next day.

"What have you decided?" her mother asked as she offered Shirley a piece of toast.

"I'm going to apologize?" Shirley asked. "To Claire and to the others too? Especially Gaylord?"

"Are you asking us or telling us, Shirley?" her father asked.

"Can't I do both at the same time?"

"I'd prefer it if you told us."

"I'm going to apologize to everyone under the sun," Shirley said gravely. "I'm going to do it in person and I'm going to do it right away. If they want to throw rocks at me, they can get it over with right away too."

"It sounds like a good plan," her mother said. "It's a very mature thing to do."

"Throwing rocks?" Shirley asked, horrified. "At me?"

"I meant the other stuff, Shirley," Mrs. Garfield said. "Don't worry about the rocks part."

Shirley picked up her book bag and her purse and let herself out of the house. She wished her parents hadn't been smiling.

When Shirley arrived at New Eden Middle, there were only a few cars parked in the faculty parking lot and none of the school buses had arrived. That was just what she had hoped. She needed a head start if she was going to get everything done as quickly and painlessly as possible.

Shirley sat down on the front steps and waited. She saw Mr. and Mrs. Simkins drive in and park their car. She also saw them kissing each other before they got out. For a second she wished she had someone to tell about it later on. But since Shirley didn't have a friend in the world, there wasn't much likelihood of that ever happening.

After the Simkinses had said good morning to Shirley and disappeared into the school, she heard what she had been waiting for. It was the school bus and she could hear the screaming of the kids before she saw the bus itself. It was one of the reasons Shirley was glad to walk to school. The noise inside was deafening and always would be because Mr. Callahan, the driver, refused to get his hearing aid fixed.

She stood up as the bus pulled up along the curb. She searched the windows for one face in particular. As Shirley might have predicted, Claire was standing at the front of the bus. Claire was always the first one to get off.

"Oh, Claire," she said as soon as Claire's feet had landed on the curb, "I have to speak to you."

"Oh, it's you, Shirley," Claire said as though she hadn't seen Shirley in twenty years and was having trouble recognizing her. "What on earth are you doing here?"

"I go to school here," Shirley said. "Remember?"

"Of course I do," Claire said. "I just didn't know you had the kind of guts it takes to show up after what happened."

"What I wanted to say was that I apologize," Shirley stammered.

"Could you say that a little more clearly," Claire said. "So I can understand."

"What I wanted to say was that I apologize," Shirley repeated so that Claire and practically all the other kids who had got off the bus could hear.

"Don't be embarrassed," Claire said. "It takes a big person to accept an apology. So I accept. Now would you mind getting out of my way? I've got some things to do before class begins. For one thing I've got to get my poster up on the bulletin board," Claire said as she unrolled the poster she held in her hand.

Shirley looked at it. "The Claire Van Kemp Civic Responsibility Club," Shirley read aloud. "Claire Van Kemp President. Memberships now being considered. Contact Claire Van Kemp, Admissions Committee Chairperson."

"You wouldn't happen to have a couple of extra thumbtacks on you by any chance," Claire asked.

Shirley shook her head.

"I thought you might have some in your purse," Claire said. "I thought it might be good for something."

All at once the only thing Shirley wanted to apologize to Claire for was apologizing to her in the first place, but Claire was too quick for her. Before Shirley could say another word, Claire had pushed her out of the way and was marching up the steps.

11

To Forgive Is Not Divine

Shirley stood on the steps watching Claire walk into the school. Even if she lived to be a hundred, she would never forgive herself for having tried to be nice to someone as mean as Claire Van Kemp.

The musketeers' case, however, was something else again. Shirley wasn't about to let Claire's meanness get in the way of apologizing to them. Shirley looked around for them, but they were nowhere in sight. In fact, no one who went to New Eden Middle was anywhere in sight. They had all gone into the school. Shirley heard the first bell ring and scampered up the stairs.

It wasn't until lunch that Shirley got her chance. When she got to the cafeteria, Kimberly and Margie and Gracie were already sitting at their usual table.

"Hi, girls," Shirley said in her friendliest voice.

The musketeers looked up at Shirley, but they weren't smiling.

"Look, girls," Shirley said. "I really want to apologize to all of you for what happened on Friday. I want to apologize to Gracie especially. The invitation Gaylord got was really meant for you. I feel awful about your not getting it. I feel even worse about your being so upset."

"That's what Kimmy and Margie told me," Gracie said.

"It was just horrible," Shirley went on. "But it was a perfectly honest mistake. You can understand that, can't you?"

"Because Gaylord and I have the same initials and all," Gracie said. "Kimmy and Margie explained that to me too."

"Then you'll forgive me, Gracie?" Shirley asked. "And Margie and Kim, you'll forgive me too?"

"Well, I'll forgive you if Gracie forgives you," Margie said.

"I'll go along with that," Kim said. "If Gracie can forgive you, there's no reason Margie and I shouldn't do the same."

Shirley returned her glance to Gracie. "Then you'll accept my apology, Gracie?" she asked as she put on her bravest little smile.

"Sure, I will," Gracie said as she took another bite from her tuna fish sandwich. "I know you didn't mean to make me cry."

"So that means you'll all forgive me?" Shirley asked. Having a simple conversation with the musketeers was turning into a major negotiation, Shirley thought. She wanted to get it over as soon as possible.

"We all forgive you," Margie said.

"I second the motion," Kimberly said.

"Thank you, girls," Shirley said. "Then I can be your friend again?"

"Sure thing," said Gracie.

Kimberly and Margie nodded their agreement and Shirley's brave little smile turned into a real one.

"You know, just because the club isn't a secret anymore doesn't mean we can't still have one. We can start it up again and you can be the first members."

The musketeers stopped chewing on their sandwiches.

"Gosh, Shirley," Margie said. "I don't think so. The three of us are going to be pretty busy this year. I don't think we're going to have time for another club."

"Another club?" Shirley asked. "What other club?"

"The Civic Responsibility Club," all three musketeers said in unison.

Shirley forgot any attempt to keep any kind of smile on her face. "Claire's club?" she asked. "You joined Claire's club?"

"She made us charter members, Shirley," Gracie said.

"And we meet five days a week so there really isn't much time for anything else this year," Kimberly added.

"But you don't like Claire Van Kemp," Shirley asked. "Why on earth would you join her club?"

"Well, until Friday we didn't want to join any club," Margie said. "But then you got us all excited about the idea."

"Then your club fell through," Kimberly said.

"So we joined Claire's," Gracie said. "You're not mad at us, are you, Shirley? Maybe we could get Claire to let you join too."

It was a suggestion that Shirley didn't have to think over at all. "I'm never going to speak to Claire again for the rest of my life."

"Well, if you feel that way," Gracie said, "we won't ask Claire to ask you to join."

As Shirley walked toward the counter to pick up her sandwich and a carton of chocolate milk, she decided that she didn't much care if she never spoke to the musketeers again either. As far as she was concerned, the three musketeers should have been renamed the three blind mice.

Or better yet, the three blind rats.

The last straw was Gaylord. During the morning Shirley noticed his seat was empty. During the afternoon it was still empty. Which meant that Shirley would just have to go over to the Skillmans' after school and apologize to him there.

"Hi, Shirley," Mrs. Skillman said as she opened the front door.

"I've come to see Gaylord," Shirley said. "He wasn't in school today. He's not sick or anything, is he?"

"Oh, no, Shirley," Mrs. Skillman said. "Gaylord's fine."

"That's good. May I talk to him?"

"I'm sorry, Shirley, but I'm afraid you can't."

"He didn't move back to Europe, did he?"

"Oh, no, but he has moved. That's why you can't see him."

"Where would he move?" Shirley asked. "Gaylord hardly knows anyone in New Eden except you and Mr. Skillman."

"Well, dear, it's a little hard for me to explain, but Gaylord has moved into the attic."

"Can't you tell him I'm here?"

"It wouldn't make any difference," Mrs. Skillman said. "Gaylord has locked himself in there and he says he's never coming out. That's why he missed school today."

"Oh, Mrs. Skillman," Shirley said. "It's all my fault. I did something I didn't mean to do and that's why he's up there. You've got to make him come out so I can apologize."

"I don't think anything could make Gaylord come out," Mrs. Skillman said. "Don't take it too badly, Shirley. He told me all about what happened on Friday and I explained it was just a mistake."

"Then why is he in the attic?"

"Gaylord has a lot of thinking to catch up on,"

she said. "If he ever comes down, I'll tell him you were here."

"Thank you, Mrs. Skillman. I'd appreciate that."

"Please, Shirley, don't be too hard on yourself. Gaylord has to start growing up just the way everyone else has to."

By the time Shirley got back to her own house, she realized that she had no idea what Mrs. Skillman had been talking about. Besides, she was much too tired from apologizing to everyone to try to figure it out.

She felt so tired that she decided to take a nap. When she woke up, though, she felt even more tired than she had before. But at least she didn't feel sorry for anyone else anymore. She didn't feel sorry for the musketeers and she certainly didn't feel sorry for Claire, and she didn't feel sorry for Gaylord. If he wanted to live in an attic, that was what he deserved.

There was only one person in the world Shirley felt sorry for. That was herself. After a while she decided that feeling sorry for yourself was a lot more worthwhile than feeling sorry for other people.

12

The Terrible Truth

For a whole month Shirley felt sorry for herself. She felt sorry for herself when she woke up in the morning and she felt sorry for herself all through school too. When she got home, she devoted a little more time to feeling sorry for herself. She even felt sorry for herself at bedtime when she put out her clothes for the next day.

The most painful times were when she passed Claire with the musketeers following behind. As soon as she saw them coming, she looked away so they couldn't say hello to her even if they wanted to, which Shirley knew they didn't. If Shirley had to, she was perfectly prepared to go on having lunch by herself and sitting alone on the swings during recess for the rest of her life.

Four days after Gaylord went into the attic he came out. Shirley knew she should go up to him and say something, but she figured there was no point to it.

Saying something to the others had only made things worse, after all.

The very worst times, however, the times when Shirley felt sorriest for herself, were when she was passing the bulletin board in the main hall of the school. In addition to the poster for Claire's club, there were posters now for Randy Pratt's Pig-Out Club and Greg Stockard's Auto Repair Club. Every day, it seemed, there was another poster for yet another club.

"Children," she would say under her breath. "They're just a bunch of kids."

Sometimes her parents would try to talk her out of her mood. Her father tried to make her laugh, calling her mood a "blue funk." But it only made Shirley more determined to stay sorry for herself forever.

It was in October, while her blue funk was blossoming into a deep purple, that Shirley noticed for the first time that some of the leaves on the trees along Maple Avenue were beginning to turn brown and orange and gold. Some of them had even begun to fall on the sidewalks and the lawns. It wouldn't be long before the fathers of New Eden were raking up the leaves and pushing them into big piles for the little kids to jump in on Saturday afternoons.

Shirley was thinking so hard about the times her own father had made leaf piles for her when she was young that she walked past her own house. It wasn't until she saw Gaylord standing on the other side of the Skillmans' picket fence that Shirley realized her mistake. Gaylord was raking a few leaves that had fallen from the Skillmans' maple tree.

"It's Shirley Garfield, I presume," Gaylord said as he rested the rake against the trunk of the tree and began to walk toward her.

"Of course it's me, Shirley Garfield," Shirley said. Just seeing Gaylord made her feel embarrassed. His being nice made it even worse. "Who else did you think it was?"

"I was just teasing you a little," Gaylord said. "I'm sorry. It's just that I haven't seen you around much lately. Not since . . . well, you know when."

Shirley cleared her throat. "Come on, Gaylord. You can say it. You haven't seen much of me since the day I made a complete fool of myself and ruined my life forever. I suppose you think I'm responsible for ruining your life too."

"You didn't ruin my life forever," Gaylord said. "Just for a little while and I guess it wasn't really all your fault anyway, though I sure thought it was at the time."

"Well, Gaylord," Shirley said, "even if it wasn't completely my fault, I'm still sorry. How was life in the attic?"

Gaylord smiled a little bit. "I was there only for four days."

"Did your aunt and uncle finally make you come out?"

"That was the rough part," Gaylord said. "They said I could stay there as long as I wanted as long as I promised to eat and keep up with my homework. My aunt left me food in the upstairs hall."

"What did you do about . . . ?" Shirley couldn't find the right word, probably because it was the kind of question nice people don't ask.

"Oh, that," Gaylord said. "There's a little bathroom in the attic. I wouldn't have gone into hiding if there hadn't been one."

Now Gaylord was grinning. It made Shirley decide that he was even better looking than she had remembered. Since she sat three rows in back of him, she still hadn't seen much of his face in class. And outside of class she hadn't seen anyone for weeks and weeks. She liked especially the spit curl that hung down the center of his forehead. If Gaylord didn't go bald before he was fifteen, he was probably going to be what the high school girls called sexy.

"What made you come out?" Shirley asked.

"I don't know," Gaylord said. "I just got bored."

"Gosh, Gaylord, if your aunt and uncle were nice enough to feed you while you were in the attic, you probably could have got them to bring up a radio or a television. You could have held out a lot longer."

"Oh, that was no problem. I took a radio up with me and my uncle brought me a TV the second day."

"So why were you bored?"

"I got bored with myself," Gaylord said. "I guess I just got tired of feeling sorry for myself and I got bored with being mean about everyone else. And I got bored feeling mad at everyone because they belong and I don't."

"Yeah," Shirley said. "I've lived here all my life, but I know what it's like not to belong. If there was a bathroom in my mother's attic, I'd spend the rest of my life there."

"I don't see why you need to," Gaylord said. "You've sort of been living in an attic ever since your club thing."

"I don't know what on earth you're talking about," Shirley said sternly. "I haven't been doing anything of the kind."

"That's exactly what you've been doing, Shirley," Gaylord said. "You go to school but you never talk to anyone. You don't even look at anyone. When lunch-time comes around, you finish your sandwich and head out to the playground before anyone can sit with you. And then you go home and feel sorry for yourself, I bet. You didn't get to have things just the way you want them so you decided to stay in your own big attic."

Shirley couldn't look at Gaylord anymore. It wasn't like the first time when she had turned away from him. That was because he had been so rude to her. This time she was ashamed to look at him. He was telling her the truth.

"You know, just because your club hit the skids doesn't mean you can't start another if that's what you really want," Gaylord was saying. "Heck, you don't even have to start one yourself to belong to one in this town. There's a club for every occasion now. You can go to Randy Pratt's Pig-Out Club or join Marcie Lewis's Diet Club. You can do music appreciation with Arthur Lomax or learn to fix up old cars with Greg Stockard. And there's always Civic Responsibility, you know."

"I don't want to join any of them," Shirley said.

"Going to stay in your attic awhile longer?"

"Until I'm ninety," Shirley said. "Or at least until I'm old enough to go to college. Whichever comes last."

"I guess I won't be seeing you at the Halloween dance," Gaylord said.

"What Halloween dance?" Shirley asked.

"I don't see how you could have missed it. The poster for it has been up for two weeks and everyone in school is talking about it."

"I gave up looking at the bulletin board last month," Shirley said. "And I don't spend too much time listening to the kids either."

"It sounds like it's going to be a lot of fun," Gaylord said.

"I don't want to go to any more little kids' parties," Shirley said. "I've seen enough ghosts and witches and clowns to last me a lifetime thank you."

"It's not going to be like that at all," Gaylord said. "It's more like a real party."

"A real party?" Shirley asked.

"It's a theme party. Everyone has to come as someone famous in American history."

"I think my mom and dad went to one of those once," Shirley said.

"When they were kids?"

"It was last year."

"So there," Gaylord said. "It really is like a grown-up party. I'd tell you who I'm going as, but everyone is supposed to keep their costumes a secret. I thought we might even go together seeing as how we live practically next door."

"Do you know if Claire will be there?"

"I don't know why she wouldn't go," Gaylord said.

"Then I definitely won't be there," Shirley said.

"Remember what I told you about trying to have everything your own way? It's not as though you'd have to dance with her. You don't even have to talk to her if you don't want to."

"Thanks, Gaylord, but I think I'll skip the dance if you don't mind."

"Well, the offer still stands," Gaylord said. "Just in case you change your mind."

Gaylord walked back to the tree and picked up the rake. Shirley turned around slowly and began to walk toward her own house. When she had gone five steps, she stopped and turned around again. Gaylord was standing where he had been, but he wasn't raking. He was just standing there, as though he had been waiting for her to turn around.

"It wouldn't be like a real date," Shirley said. "It would be more like we were just going to a party together."

"More like we were friends," Gaylord said.

"Yes," she said. "And my dad could drive us and pick us up afterward and it would save your aunt and uncle the trip and maybe we could have some hot chocolate afterward at my house. But it wouldn't be a date, you understand, because I'm not going to start dating until . . ."

"Until you're ninety?"

"Sixteen, maybe."

"I understand," Gaylord said. "But I'm still going to look forward to it."

"So am I," Shirley said. "Good-bye, Gaylord."

"Bye, Shirley."

She turned around and started to walk back to her house. By the time she got there, she felt happier than she had for a very long time.

13

Even Bad Things
Come to an End

It was the last week of October, just five days before
Halloween, that the kids in Mrs. Simkins's sixth grade
class knew that something very serious was up. The
trouble was that not one of them, Claire Van Kemp
included, had a clue as to what it was.

The tip-off was the envelopes that all the kids in the
class had to take home to their parents. It was a month
too early for report cards so everyone knew it wasn't
that. The envelopes were all sealed shut, which meant
it wasn't an announcement of another bake sale or
raffle to raise money for the basketball team's uni-
forms. What made it even more mysterious was that
none of the other classes at New Eden Middle got
envelopes to take home.

Claire Van Kemp decided that something wonderful
was about to happen. Warren Fingler wasn't so sure.
His mother groaned when she read the letter and

handed it to him. It read, "Special Meeting of the Parents of Sixth Graders and the New Eden School Administration, Tuesday night, October 28th, eight o'clock. Subject to be announced."

"Sounds ominous," Mrs. Fingler said.

"I'm sure there's nothing to worry about," Mrs. Garfield said while she and Shirley were having dinner.

"Probably another dull evening at New Eden Middle," said Randy Pratt's mother. She had five older daughters and had been to more than her share of PTA meetings.

But no matter what the grown-ups thought the meeting was about, they all went, even Gaylord's aunt and uncle who really didn't have to go since they weren't parents.

The next morning the kids searched their parents' faces for some clue as to what had happened the night before. Some even asked, but the parents said Mrs. Simkins would explain it to the class. That was one of the things they had all agreed on.

"Sounds ominous," Warren said to Shirley as they walked into the classroom ten minutes before the first bell.

"I'm sure there's nothing to worry about," Shirley said, but in a way she hoped it was something exciting anyway.

For the first time since Warren or Shirley or Claire or Randy had gone to school, every student in the class was sitting in his or her seat five whole minutes before the bell rang.

At nine o'clock the bell rang and Mrs. Simkins walked into the classroom.

"Good morning, boys and girls," she said as she placed her briefcase on her desk.

"Good morning, Mrs. Simkins," everyone said all at once, just the way it's supposed to happen but never does.

Mrs. Simkins opened her briefcase and pulled out a wad of papers. Some of the kids in the front row angled their heads to get a look at what the papers were, but not one of them could see anything.

"Maybe some of you know that there was a meeting here last night," Mrs. Simkins said. She smiled. "I guess *all* of you know about the meeting."

"But we don't know what the meeting was about," Randy Pratt said.

"Not yet, anyway," Claire said from the back of the classroom.

"The meeting was about this," Mrs. Simkins said as she held up the wad of papers. "All the clubs that you have been organizing since last month."

"Is there going to be an award for the best club, Mrs. Simkins?" Claire asked without raising her hand.

"Not quite," Mrs. Simkins said. "I called the meeting last night because I wanted to see if your parents felt the same way I do about what's been going on. I'm happy to say they feel exactly as I do. I'm afraid, though, that some of you aren't going to be as happy as I am about the outcome."

Mrs. Simkins walked to Randy Pratt's desk and looked at the top piece of paper. "Randy Pratt's Pig-Out Club," she read. "Come one. Come all." Mrs. Simkins put the piece of paper on Randy's desk. "Randy, if you want to pig out, you don't need a club for it. Your mother doesn't need to have you and your fellow members eating her out of house and home and leaving her kitchen in a state of chaos. Certainly not on an organized basis. The Randy Pratt Pig-Out Club is hereby disbanded."

Mrs. Simkins looked Randy in the eye but Randy was too stunned to speak.

"So is Marcie Lewis's Diet Club," Mrs. Simkins said as she rested the next piece of paper on Marcie's desk. "With no pig-out club we probably won't be needing a diet club. Right, Marcie?"

Marcie nodded uncertainly and Mrs. Simkins walked over to Greg Stockard's desk and read the next piece of paper. "The Greg Stockard Mechanics' Club has also been outlawed. Your father didn't enjoy having to clean up his garage last weekend after you and your gang made it look like a disaster area. And he didn't like having to pay twenty-eight seventy-three to a mechanic to undo all the corrections you made on his Chevy. You and your clubmates are going to have to find something else to do with your Tuesday afternoons."

"The Warren Fingler Jockey Club," Mrs. Simkins

read before she rested the next sheet of paper on Warren's desk. "Warren, your mother thinks it's fine for you to take riding lessons. But she's not about to put up with you and your cronies tracking dirt from Mr. Guiness's stables through her living room. Horseback riding isn't a team sport and your mother aims to keep it that way. The Warren Fingler Jockey Club is a thing of the past. Okay?"

Mrs. Simkins looked at the next sheet of paper, which was almost twice as large as the others. "The Claire Van Kemp Civic Responsibility Club," she read as she strolled to the back of the classroom where Claire was sitting. "Claire, would you please tell me just what the Civic Responsibility Club does?"

"Well, Mrs. Simkins," Claire said, "the Claire Van Kemp Civic Responsibility Club is an organization made up of young overachievers who wish to foster good citizenship in our local area."

"Okay, Claire," Mrs. Simkins said. "But what does the club do?"

"Well, last week my club met at my house and we had sandwiches and then we headed downtown looking for old people."

"You wanted to make them members?" Mrs. Simkins said. "I thought your club was for young overachievers."

"We wanted to help them cross the street, Mrs. Simkins," Claire said.

"How did things turn out, Claire?"

"Well, unfortunately, New Eden doesn't seem to

have very many old people. In fact, it was the finding of our club that New Eden doesn't have nearly enough of them. We also found out that New Eden doesn't have nearly enough streets either. We're going to discuss both problems at our next meeting. Maybe we can get some old people imported from out of state. I don't know what we can do about the street situation, though."

"Very noble of you, Claire," Mrs. Simkins said.

"Thank you, Mrs. Simkins," Claire replied. "I knew that you would understand that my club, the Claire Van Kemp Civic Responsibility Club, is quite unlike the other clubs. I would like to announce that the other kids whose clubs have been disbanded should feel free to apply for membership."

"I'm sorry, Claire," Mrs. Simkins said, "but that won't be possible."

"But Mrs. Simkins," Claire said, "I feel it's my civic duty to encourage other young overachievers like myself. It's no problem."

"It *is* a problem, Claire, because your club doesn't exist anymore. It's been outlawed too."

"But my father won't hear of it," Claire said. "And he *is* the first selectman of New Eden."

"Your father was the first person to insist that your club be disbanded, Claire. Last week after your group went out on its first mission, he got calls from two irate women who had been forced to cross Main Street very much against their will." Mrs. Simkins put Claire's poster on her desk. "Better luck next time, Claire," she said.

"Old people can be very ungrateful," Claire said. "Don't think I'm not writing the governor about it."

"That's your right," Mrs. Simkins said. "And we all have to exercise our rights. But your parents have to exercise their responsibilities, and I have to exercise my responsibilities as your teacher too. In the last month the grades in this class have hit an all-time low. I think it has a lot to do with your spending so much time on the clubs. But that's not the only problem. You kids have let the clubs get out of hand. Clubs should make people feel as though they belong. Your clubs have the reverse effect. They make a few people feel like they belong, but they make everyone else feel as though they don't. It's not fair. And it's not kind either. No one *has* to join a club but everyone ought to feel they can if they want to. The next time you start making up clubs, you ought to think about that. Until you're old enough to understand that, your parents and I don't think you're old enough to have clubs in the first place."

Mrs. Simkins paused. It was as though she was waiting for a collective groan from the class. There was none. "Are there any questions?" she asked. "Otherwise, I think we should get back to our schoolwork."

Shirley raised her hand.

"Yes, Shirley. What would you like to add?"

"I just wanted to know if we were still going to have

the Halloween party at the end of the week?" she asked.

"Of course we are," Mrs. Simkins said. "It's not that we're trying to outlaw fun."

"I think it's very unfair," Claire said more to herself than to anyone else.

Everyone looked back to see Claire still fuming in her seat.

Maybe life was unfair sometimes, Shirley thought, but this was one time when she didn't seem to mind.

14

The Dance

When the kids of New Eden have the rotten luck to have the first of September fall on a Monday, there is some compensation at least in the fact that Halloween will fall on a Friday. Even in New Eden Friday is not a school night, and that meant that the Halloween party would last until nine o'clock instead of eight.

When Mrs. Simkins announced later on in the day that some committees would be needed to make the party a rousing success, the sixth grade perked up. Committees weren't clubs exactly but they were a close second. Right away Randy Pratt volunteered to work on the Refreshments Committee and the musketeers said they wanted to be the Decorations Committee. Arthur Lomax said he would find records for them to play and Greg Stockard volunteered to bring his stereo from home. Warren Fingler said he would arrange games.

Five days wasn't very much time to arrange everything, but by Friday night everyone agreed that their efforts had been heroic. With orange and black streamers blanketing the ceiling, pumpkins in both basketball hoops, paper skeletons on all the walls, and candles on all the tables, the gym looked almost like a haunted house. The musketeers had outdone themselves.

Nor had Randy Pratt stinted on the refreshments. Three tables with food had been set up and everything tasted as wonderful as it looked. On each table there were pitchers of cider and bowls of apples and plates of donuts. Randy's only misgiving was that all the food was wholesome. There wasn't a greasy hamburger in the whole place, but since everyone else seemed to think it was all terrific, Randy didn't mind too much.

If Shirley Garfield had had the time, she would have volunteered for one of the committees. As it was, she had barely enough time to put her own costume together.

Over the weekend she had gone to the library and brought home books to make sure that her costume looked absolutely authentic. On Monday she and her mother had bought the material and the next three nights they sewed it all together. By Thursday, when Shirley put the costume on for the first time, everything was perfect. Even her mother agreed that she looked exactly like the drawings of Martha Washington they had seen in the library books. Shirley had a gray bonnet and she had a beautiful gray dress that fell all the way down to her ankles. And her mother had sewn lovely old lace around the collar and the cuffs. She even had a wig. As she admired herself in the mirror, her only regret was that she didn't have a purse to go with the costume. But none of the portraits had shown Martha with a purse, and Shirley wasn't about to do anything that wasn't truly authentic.

At seven o'clock Mr. Garfield drove Shirley over to the Skillmans' house to pick up Gaylord.

"How do I look?" he asked as he got into the backseat of the car.

"You're a spaceman," Shirley exclaimed. "You look wonderful, Gaylord."

"I'm not just any spaceman," Gaylord said. "I'm John Glenn. I'm the first American spaceman. You look wonderful too, Shirley. You're Martha Washington. You're perfect."

Shirley beamed. You couldn't do better than perfect, after all.

When she and Gaylord walked into the school gym, the party had already begun. As Shirley looked around, she had to admit that practically everyone else looked perfect too. But she felt so good about herself that she didn't mind.

Standing at one of the refreshment tables, Randy Pratt was all dressed up as Benjamin Franklin. In one hand he was holding a kite. In the other he was holding two donuts.

"After I finish these donuts, I'm going to discover electricity. Better stand back, everybody," he said. "I don't want any of you to be shocked. Get it? Shocked?"

Shirley got it and laughed a little. Then she turned

to look around some more. Not too far away were the musketeers. Except they weren't the musketeers tonight. Kimberly had come as Susan B. Anthony and she had a placard reading "Women's Suffrage Now" to prove it. Margie was wearing an old-fashioned nurse uniform, cap and all, plus a blue cape so you could tell she was Clara Barton. Gracie Arnold was all dressed up as an Indian.

"I'm Pocahontas in case you couldn't tell," Gracie said.

"You look just like her," Shirley said.

"I love your Martha Washington costume," Gracie said.

"Thank you," replied Shirley as she looked around the room some more.

Over in one corner Davy Crockett was talking to E.T., only it was really Greg Stockard and Warren Fingler. Shirley wasn't sure that E.T. counted as a figure in American history, but she thought the costume was cute anyway.

Then Shirley saw a figure standing by himself under one of the basketball hoops. It was George Washington, but Shirley couldn't tell who it really was. As she walked a little closer to find out, George looked at her. It seemed he didn't know who she was either.

Then Shirley stopped in her tracks. George Washington was no one else but Claire Van Kemp. And George wasn't any happier about seeing that Martha was Shirley than Shirley was about seeing that George was Claire. Never before in history had George and

Martha Washington given each other such dirty looks.

Now everyone else in the gym was staring at Claire and Shirley as they stared at each other. Shirley took a step toward Claire and Claire took a step toward Shirley.

"How dare you come as Martha Washington?" Claire demanded.

"You've got some nerve coming as George Washington," Shirley shouted back. "If I had a glass of cider, I'd throw it at you."

"Just a second, Shirley," Randy Pratt said. "I'll get you some cider. You want some too, Claire?" Of all the people at the dance Randy was the only one who seemed to enjoy seeing the mother and father of his country on the verge of a fight.

But before Randy could move, Mrs. Simkins was making her way through the crowd.

"Children, children," she said, a little nervously, as she put one hand on Claire's shoulder and the other hand on Shirley's. "Isn't this just the nicest party we've ever had? I'm so pleased everyone could come and I'm so impressed with all your costumes. But this is a dance, children, and no one is dancing. I think it would be nice if George and Martha led off the first dance, don't you?"

"I don't want to dance," George said. "Not with her."

"I absolutely refuse," Martha said.

"Don't be silly," Mrs. Simkins said. "George and Martha Washington always danced together."

"If I dance with anyone, I'm going to dance with John Glenn," Martha Washington said.

"I was thinking about asking Davy Crockett to dance," George Washington said.

"No, you won't," Mrs. Simkins said. "Martha Washington never danced with John Glenn. And George never danced with Davy. Haven't you two been following any of our history lessons?"

"To tell you the truth, Mrs. Simkins, I'd rather die," George said.

"For once I agree," Martha said.

"Well, if you won't dance together at least once, I'm going to have to flunk you both in history," Mrs. Simkins said cheerfully. "Would you rather flunk than dance?"

"You wouldn't do that to us, Mrs. Simkins, would you?" Claire asked.

"Don't tempt me, Claire," Mrs. Simkins said. "You, either, Shirley. I've had it with your feud. I'm not going to put up with it another second."

George Washington took a deep breath. "Okay," she said. "One dance and that's it. But I'm going to lead. You tell her that, Mrs. Simkins."

"Oh, no, you won't," Martha said. "I'm going to be doing the leading."

"I'm sure that you'll figure something out," Mrs. Simkins said. "Greg, would you put on the music please?"

Greg Stockard turned on the stereo. Very slowly, George held out her arms and so did Martha. A second later the mother and father of their country were dancing.

And although no one could ever explain it afterward, both George and Martha were leading.

15

What Happened Last

Shirley decided that the best thing she could say about the whole dance was that she had managed to live through it. But later on, when she and Gaylord were sipping hot chocolate in the Garfields' kitchen, she had to admit that things had turned out better than that. Besides, she couldn't blame anyone, even Claire, for the fact that they had come as America's first couple.

She thought about what Gaylord had said to her about not being happy unless everything worked out your way all the time. Just because things don't work out exactly as you planned doesn't mean everything is terrible.

It was just a beginning, Shirley knew. Maybe it even had something to do with being a real grown-up. But Shirley would think about that the next day. Right now she was having too nice a time sitting with Gaylord and talking with him and drinking hot chocolate to worry about it.

And that, Shirley Garfield realized to her own surprise, was the way things probably should be.